GUARDIANS OF THE GALAXY

ROCKET RACCOON™ #5

STORYTAILER

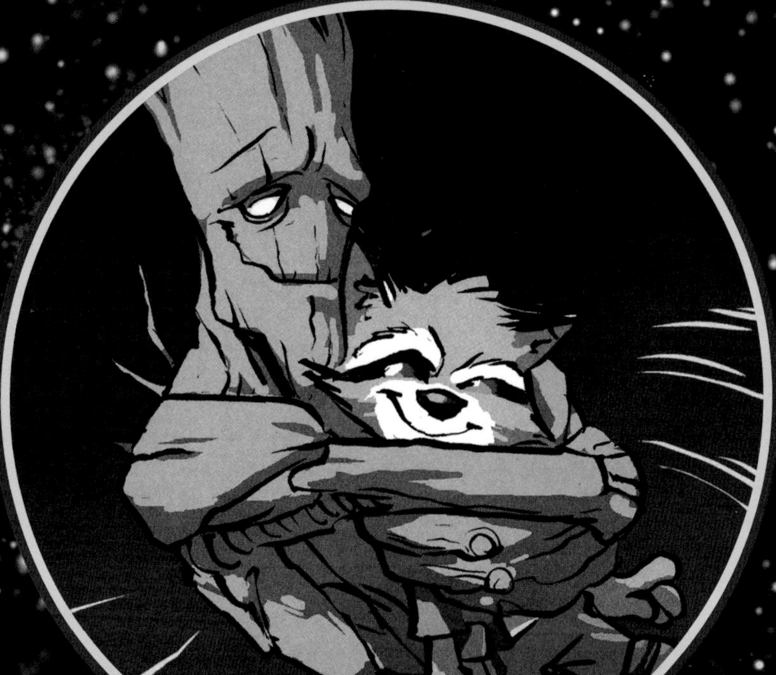

MARVEL
marvelkids.com

ABDO
Spotlight

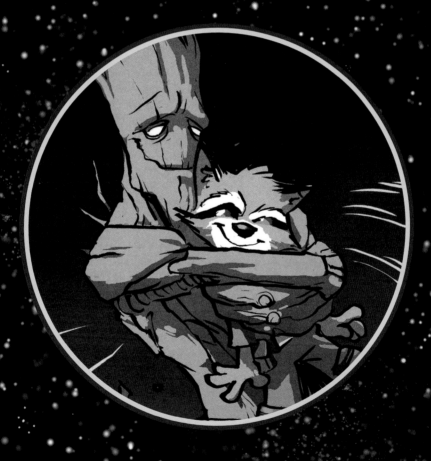

ABDOPUBLISHING.COM

Reinforced library bound edition published in 2018 by Spotlight,
a division of ABDO, PO Box 398166, Minneapolis, Minnesota 55439.
Spotlight produces high-quality reinforced library bound editions for
schools and libraries. Published by agreement with Marvel Characters, Inc.

Printed in the United States of America, North Mankato, Minnesota.
042017
092017

THIS BOOK CONTAINS
RECYCLED MATERIALS

marvelkids.com
© 2017 MARVEL

PUBLISHER'S CATALOGING IN PUBLICATION DATA

Names: Young, Skottie, author. | Young, Skottie ; Beaulieu, Jean-Francois ; Parker, Jake, illustrators.
Title: Rocket Raccoon / writer: Skottie Young ; art: Skottie Young ; Jean-Francois Beaulieu ; Jake Parker.
Description: Reinforced library bound edition. | Minneapolis, Minnesota : Spotlight, 2018. | Series: Guardians of the galaxy : Rocket Raccoon | Volumes 1, 2, 3, and 4 written by Skottie Young ; illustrated by Skottie Young & Jean-Francois Beaulieu. | Volumes 5 and 6 written by Skottie Young ; illustrated by Skottie Young , Jake Parker & Jean-Francois Beaulieu.
Summary: Rocket's high-flying life of adventure is at stake when he's framed for murder, and with an imposter one step ahead of him, and various terminators tracking him, can Rocket make it out alive and clear his name?
Identifiers: LCCN 2017931597 | ISBN 9781532140846 (#1: A Chasing Tale Part One) | ISBN 9781532140853 (#2: A Chasing Tale Part Two) | ISBN 9781532140860 (#3: A Chasing Tale Part Three) | ISBN 9781532140877 (#4: A Chasing Tale Part Four) | ISBN 9781532140884 (#5: Storytailer) | ISBN 9781532140891 (#6: Misfit Mechs)
Subjects: LCSH: Superheroes--Juvenile fiction. | Adventure and adventurers--Juvenile fiction. | Comic books, strips, etc.--Juvenile fiction. | Graphic novels--Juvenile fiction.
Classification: DDC 741.5--dc23
LC record available at https://lccn.loc.gov/2017931597

Spotlight

A Division of ABDO
abdopublishing.com

MARVEL ENTERTAINMENT PROUDLY PRESENTS

ROCKET

GUARDIAN OF THE GALAXY, GUNSLINGER, GROWN-UP?!

AFTER WEEKS TRACKING AN INIQUITOUS IMPOSTER POSING AS ANOTHER RACCOON, ROCKET FOUND HIMSELF FACE-TO-FACE WITH NONE OTHER THAN BLACKJACK O'HARE, A MERCILESS MERCENARY!

NOT ONLY THAT, BUT A GROUP OF KILLER EX-GIRLFRIENDS FINALLY CAUGHT UP TO THE BOTH OF THEM AND WANTED TO THROW DOWN!

ROCKET BARELY MADE IT OUT OF THE BRAWL IN ONE PIECE (AND SUFFERED A LITTLE EMOTIONA TRAUMA ALONG THE WAY), BUT HE'S FINALLY EARNED HIMSELF A LITTLE R&R WITH HIS FELLOW GUARDIANS.

RACCOON

STORYTAILER

skottie young writer	**jake parker & skottie young** artists	**jean-françois beaulie** color art
jeff eckleberry lettering	**skottie young** cover art	**jason latour** variant cover	**idette winecoor** production
devin lewis assistant editor	**sana amanat** editor		**nick lowe** senior editor
axel alonso editor in chief	**joe quesada** chief creative officer	**dan buckley** publisher	**alan fine** executive producer

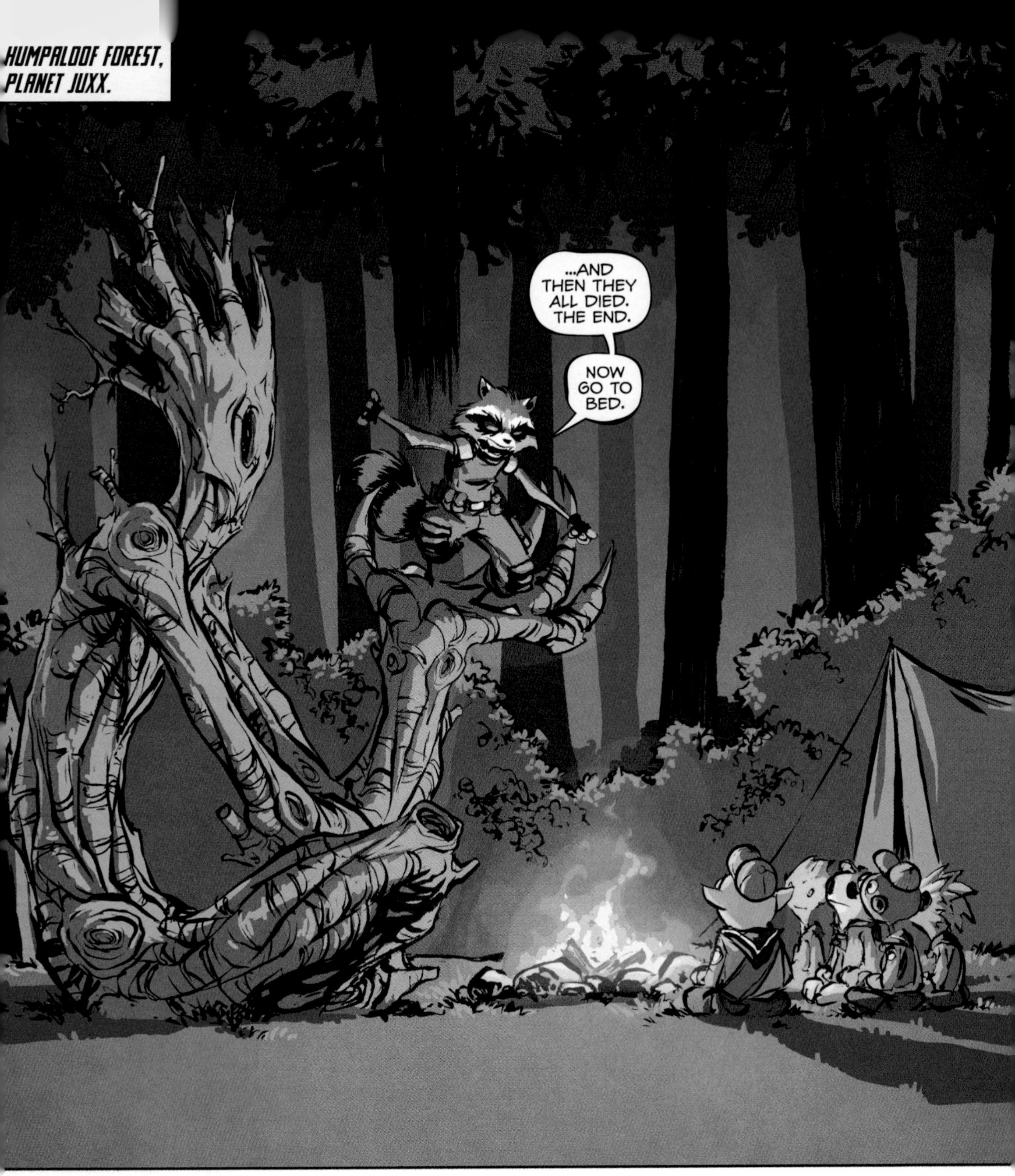
HUMPALOOF FOREST, PLANET JUXX.
...AND THEN THEY ALL DIED. THE END.
NOW GO TO BED.

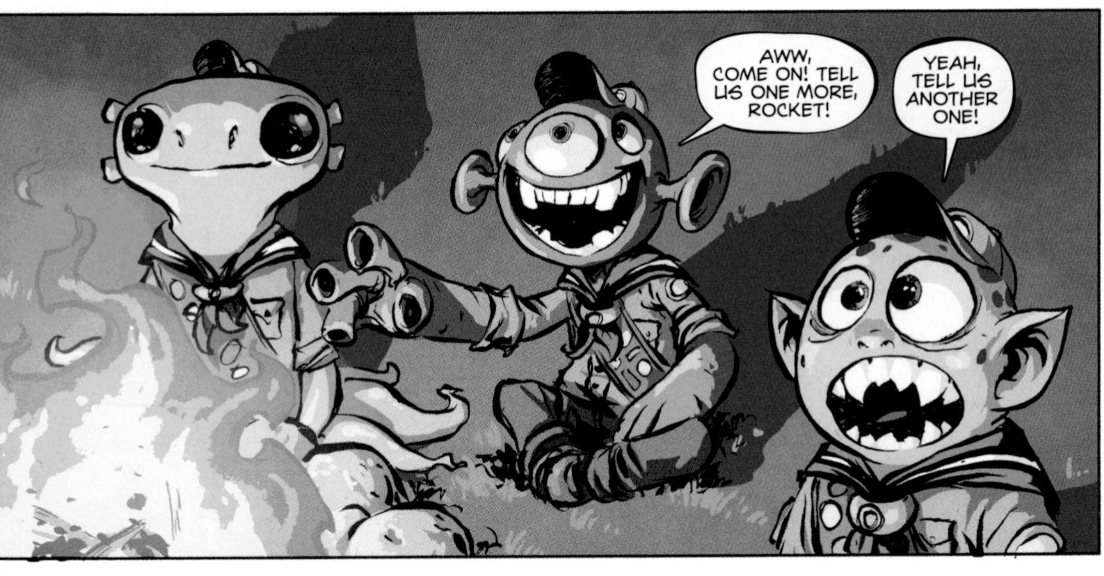
AWW, COME ON! TELL US ONE MORE, ROCKET!
YEAH, TELL US ANOTHER ONE!

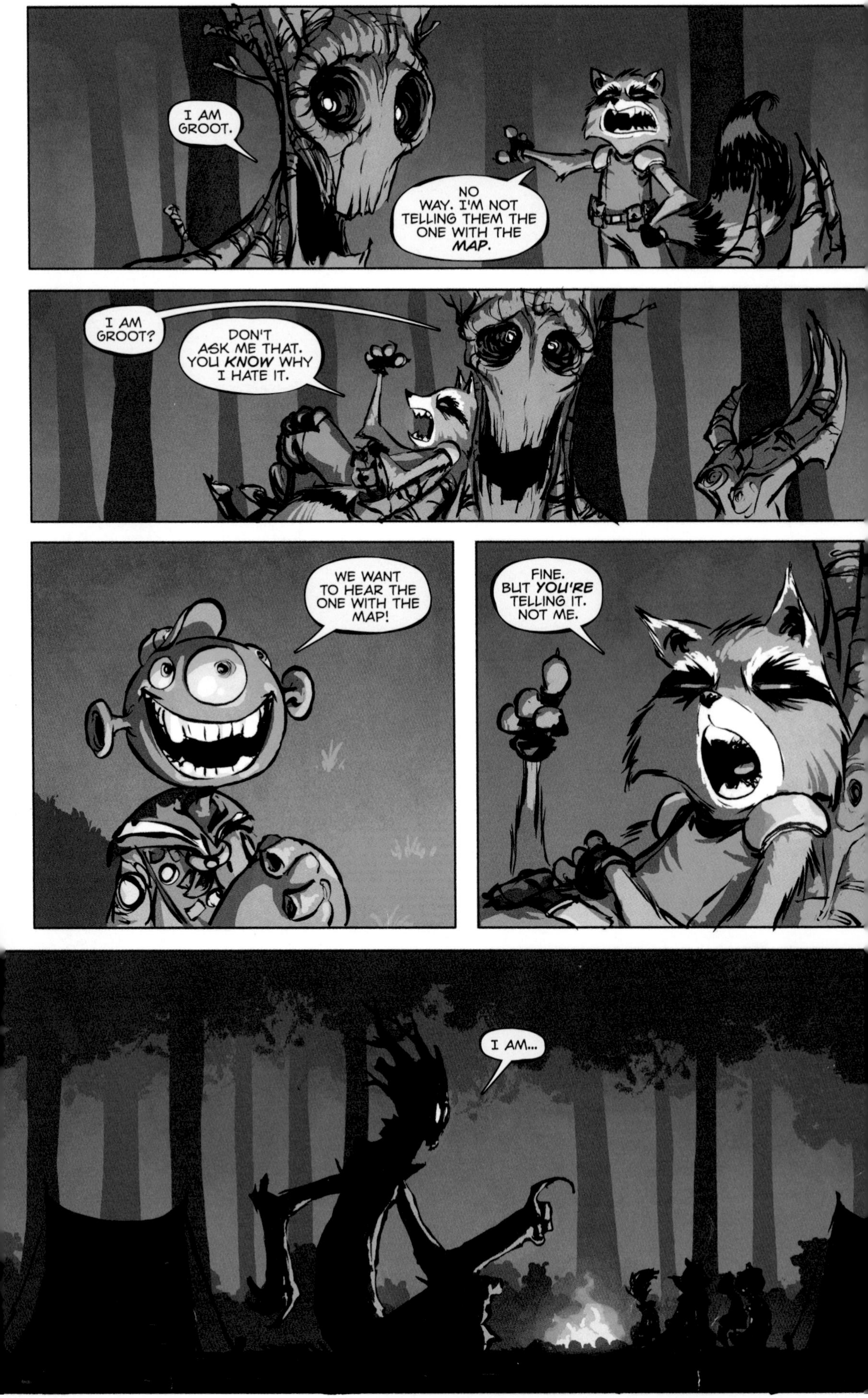
I AM GROOT.
NO WAY. I'M NOT TELLING THEM THE ONE WITH THE ***MAP***.
I AM GROOT?
DON'T ASK ME THAT. YOU ***KNOW*** WHY I HATE IT.
WE WANT TO HEAR THE ONE WITH THE MAP!
FINE. BUT ***YOU'RE*** TELLING IT. NOT ME.
I AM...

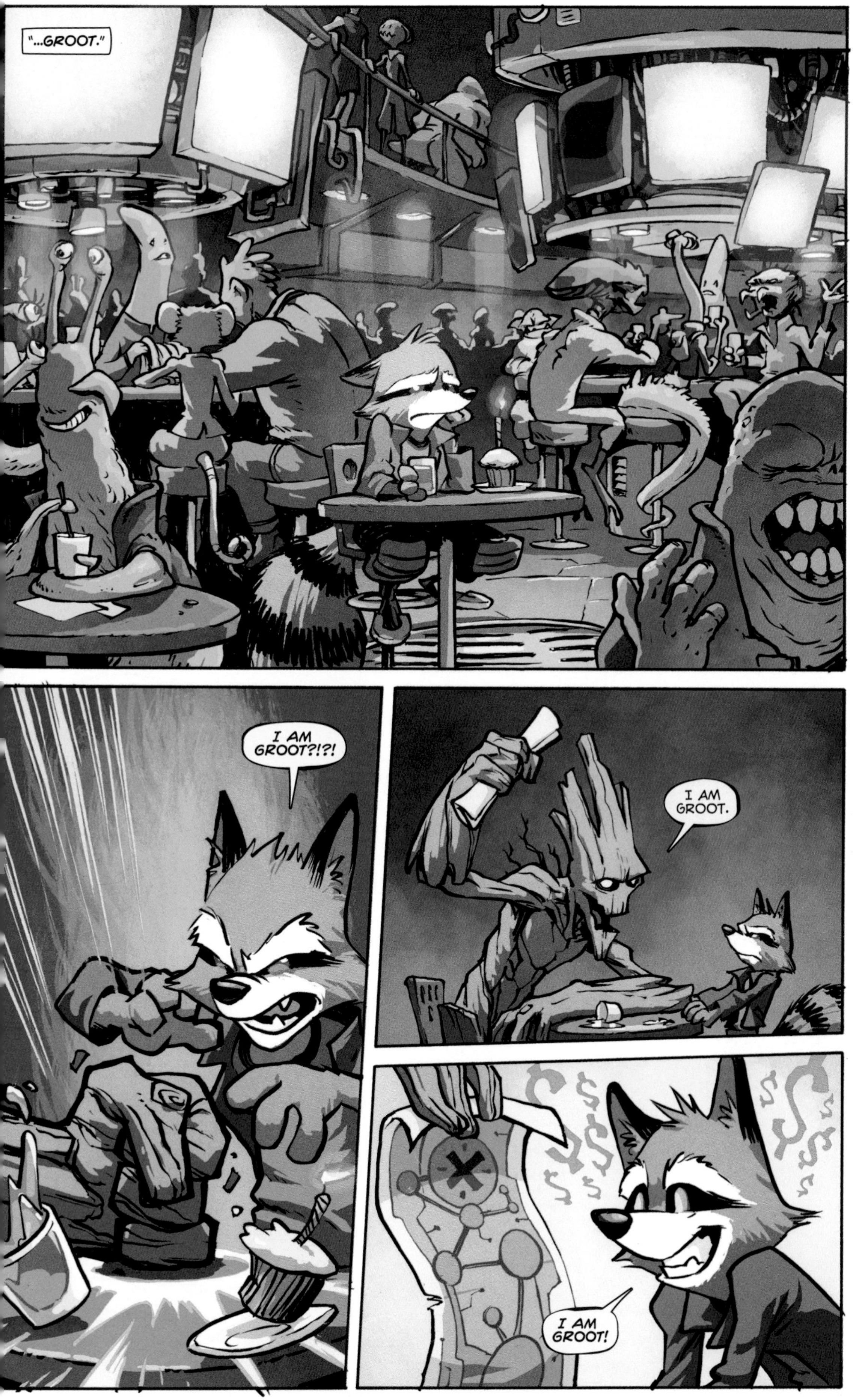
"...GROOT."
I AM GROOT?!?!
I AM GROOT.
I AM GROOT!

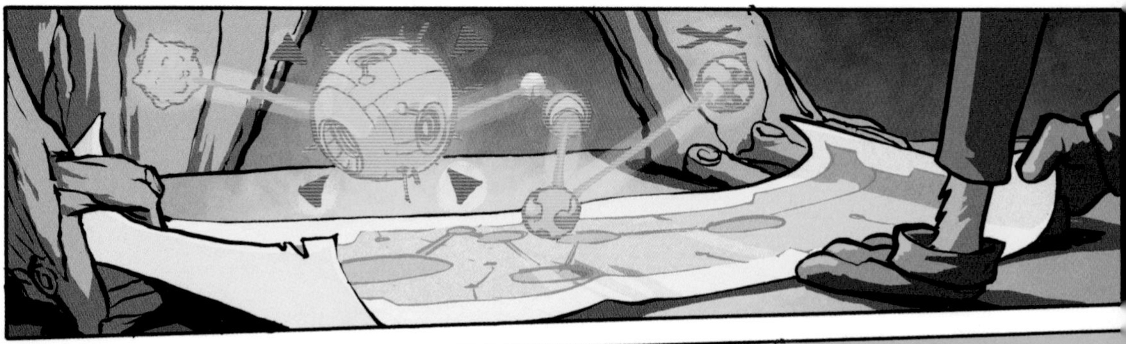

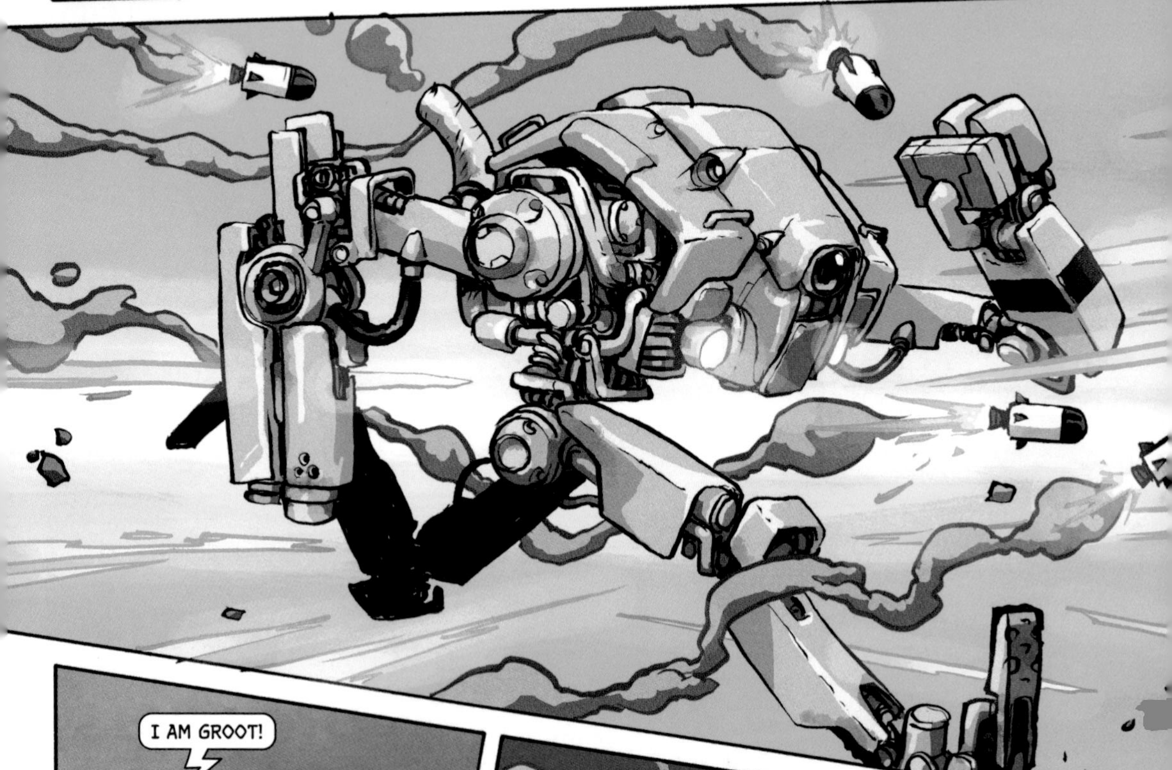

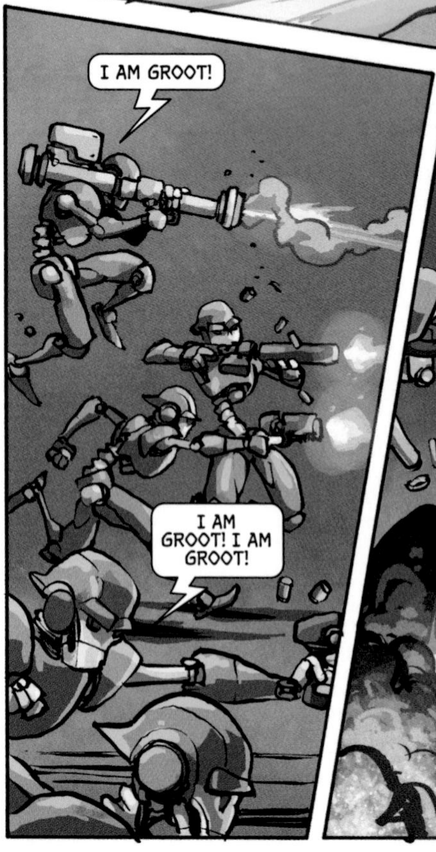
I AM GROOT!
I AM GROOT! I AM GROOT!

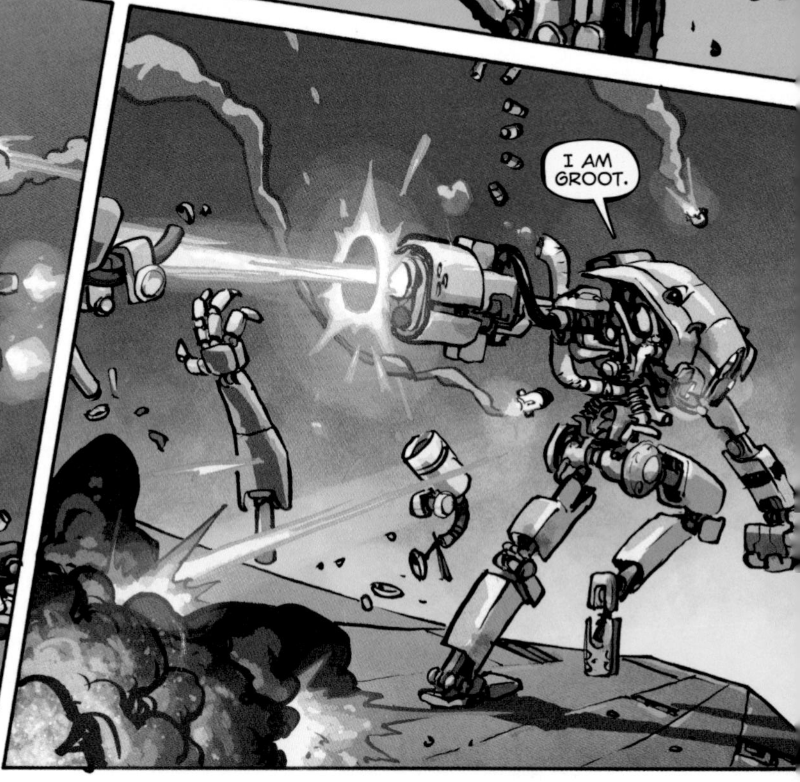
I AM GROOT.

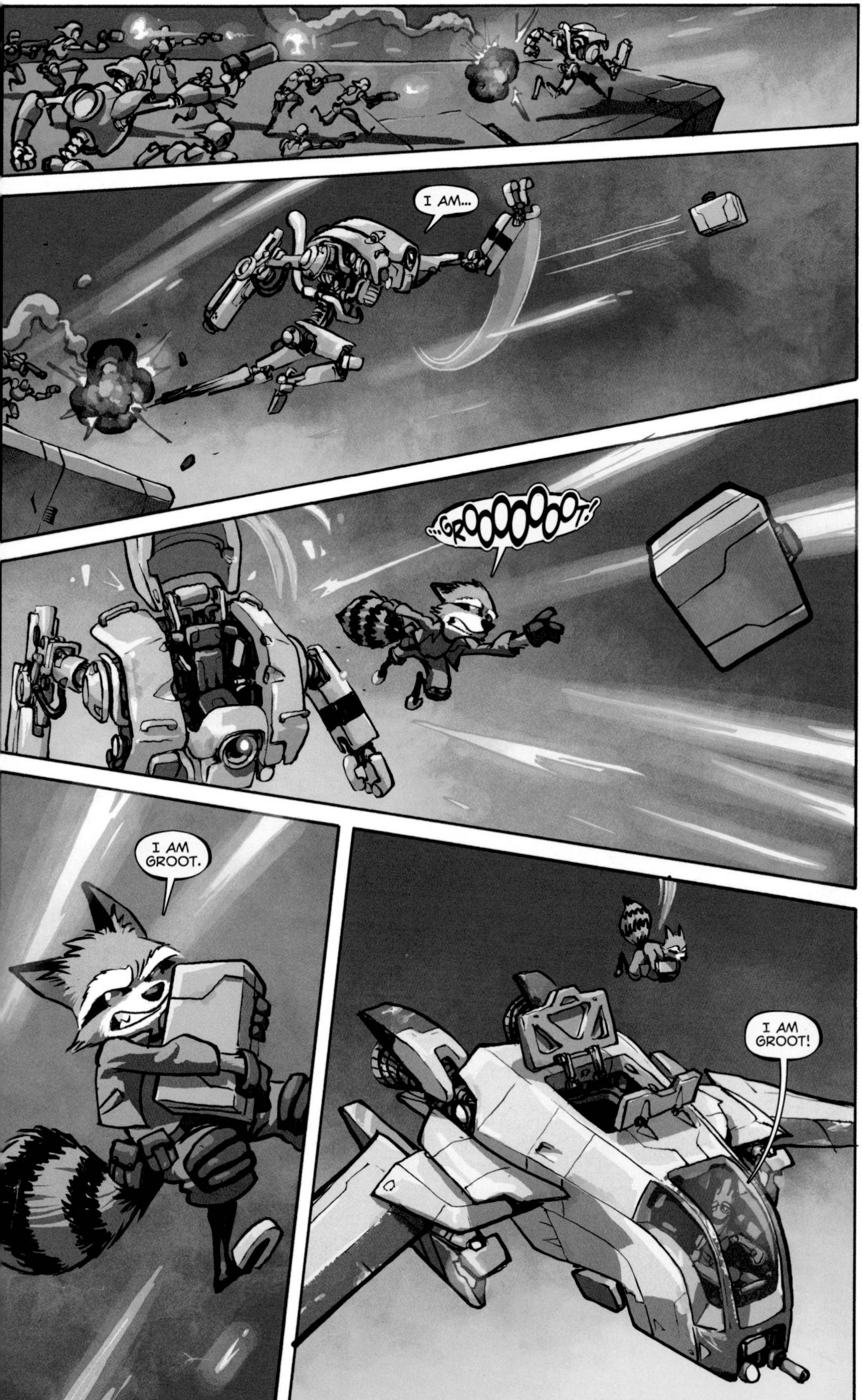

I AM...
...GROOOOOOOOT!
I AM GROOT.
I AM GROOT!

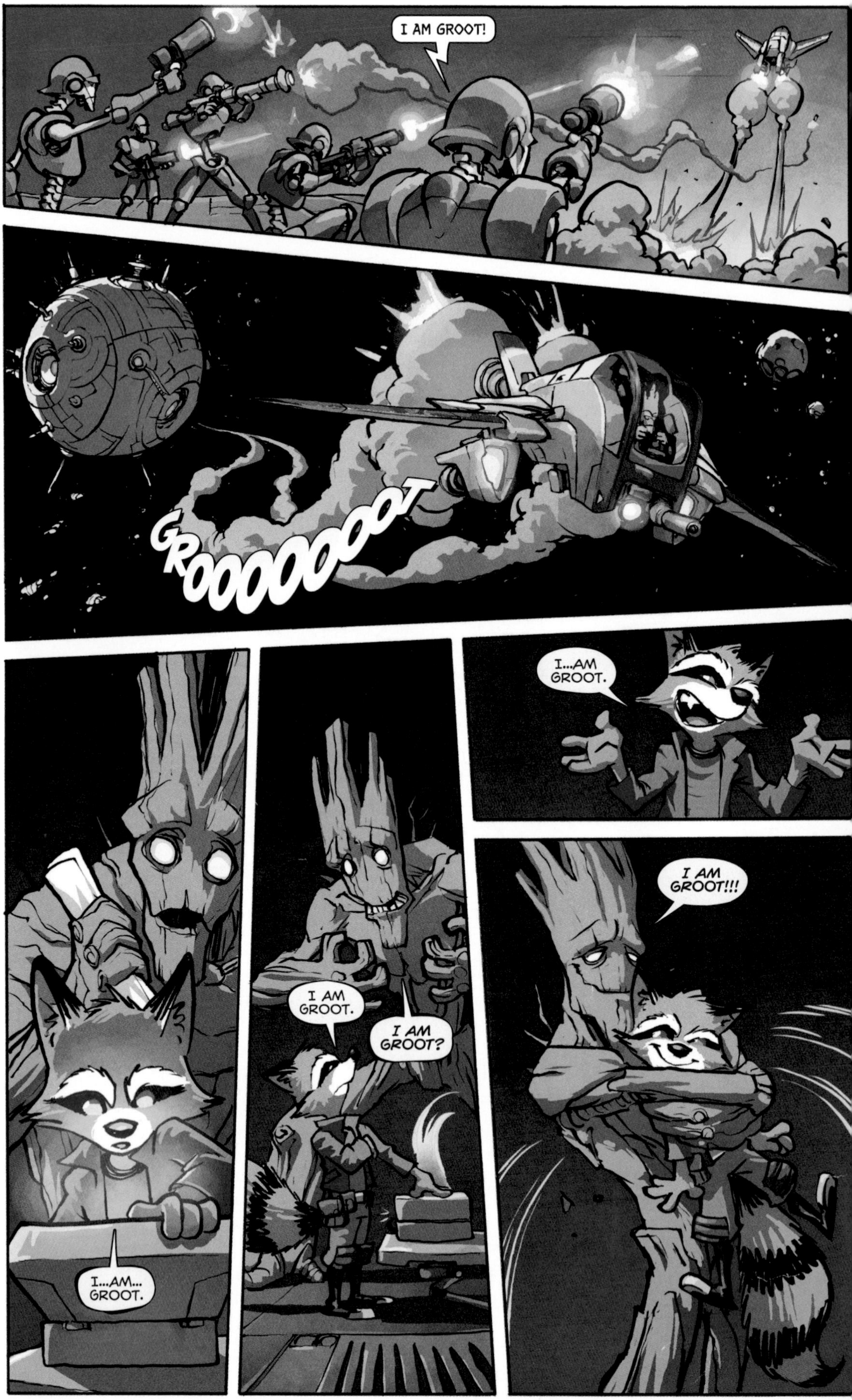
I AM GROOT!
GROOOOOOOOT
I...AM...
GROOT.
I AM
GROOT.
I AM
GROOT?
I...AM
GROOT.
I AM
GROOT!!!

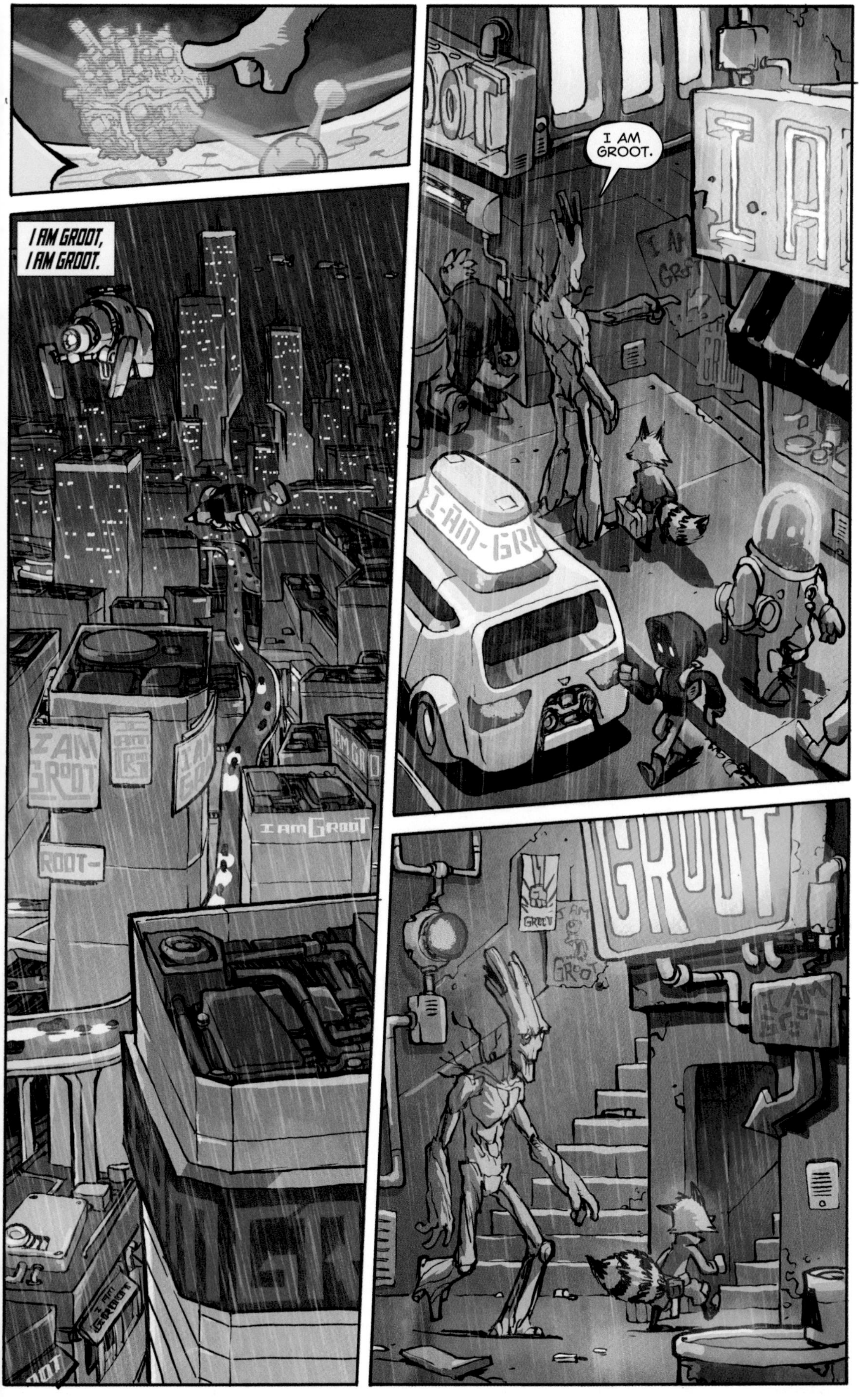
I AM GROOT,
I AM GROOT.
I AM GROOT
ROOT-
I AM GROOT.
GROOT

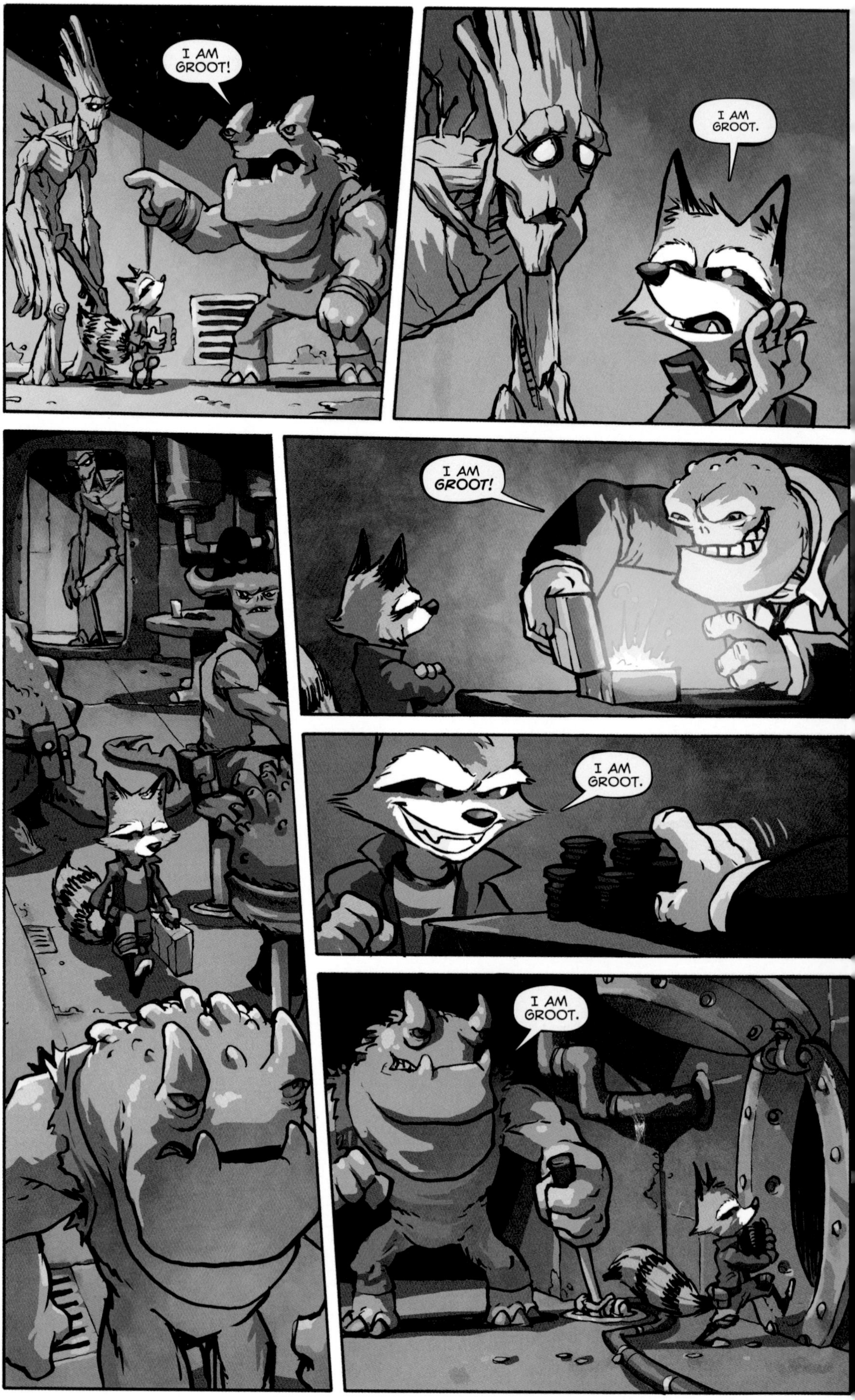
I AM GROOT!
I AM GROOT.
I AM GROOT!
I AM GROOT.
I AM GROOT.

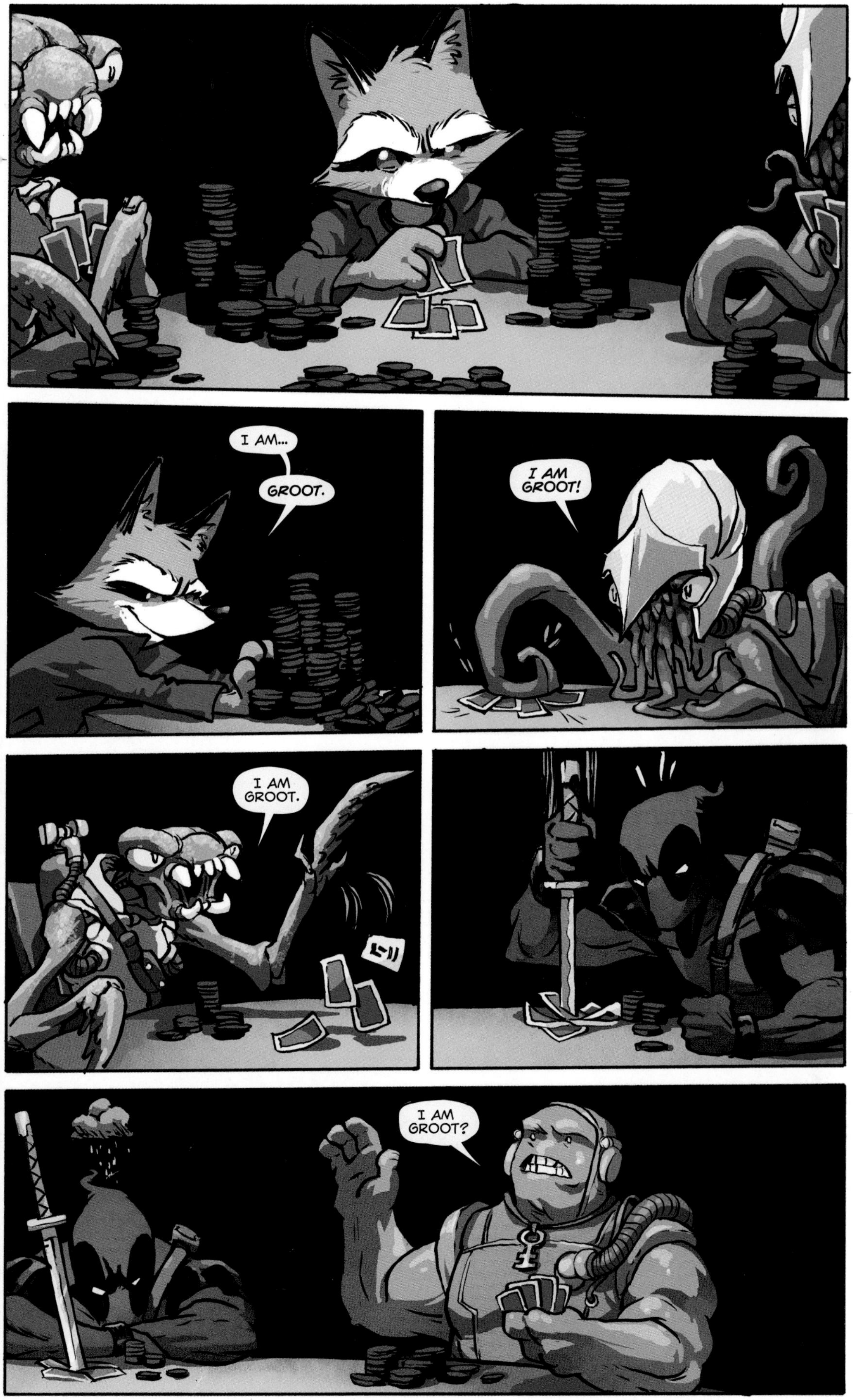
I AM...
GROOT.
I AM GROOT!
I AM GROOT.
I AM GROOT?

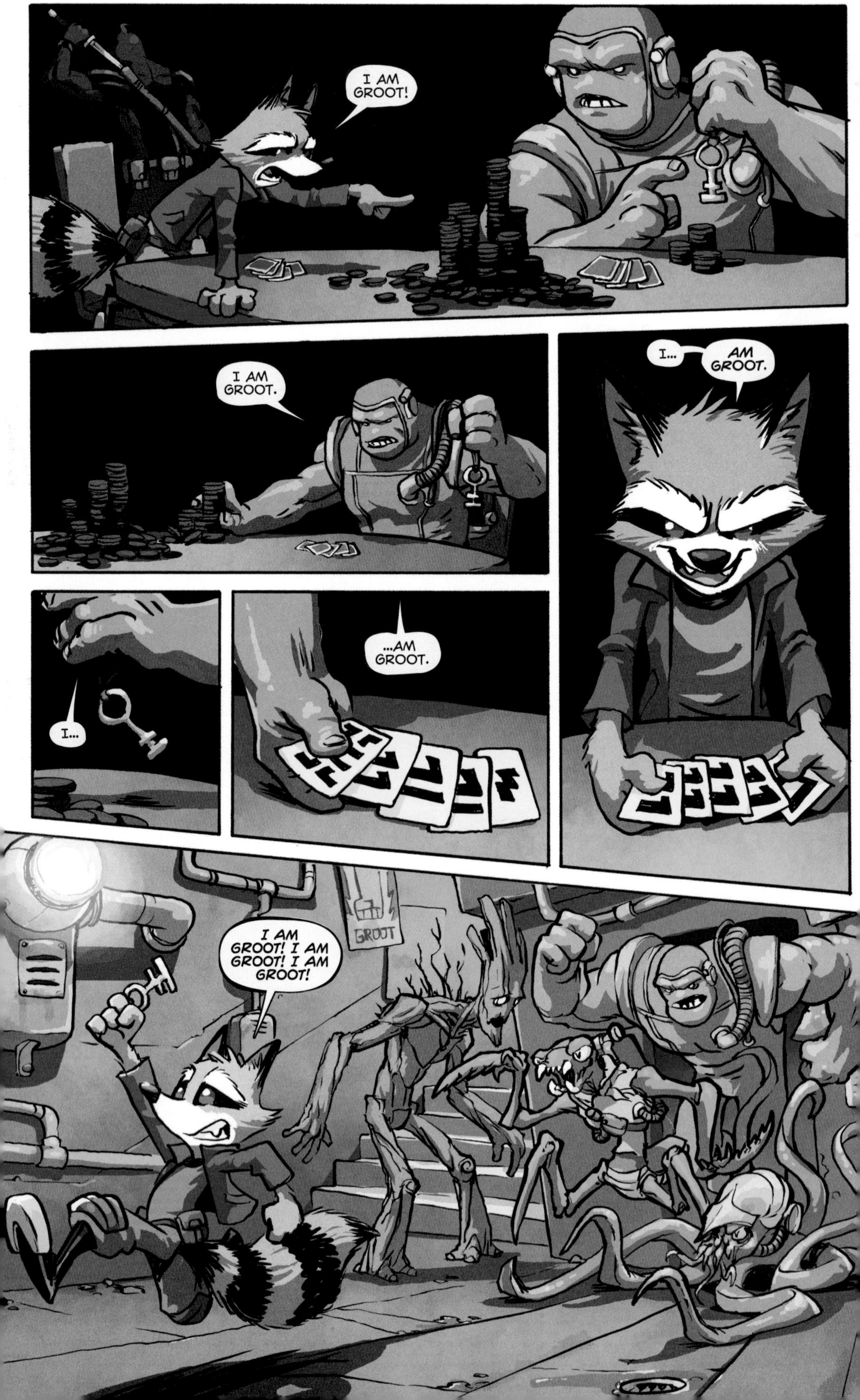
I AM GROOT!
I AM GROOT.
I...
AM GROOT.
I...
...AM GROOT.
I AM GROOT! I AM GROOT! I AM GROOT!
GROOT

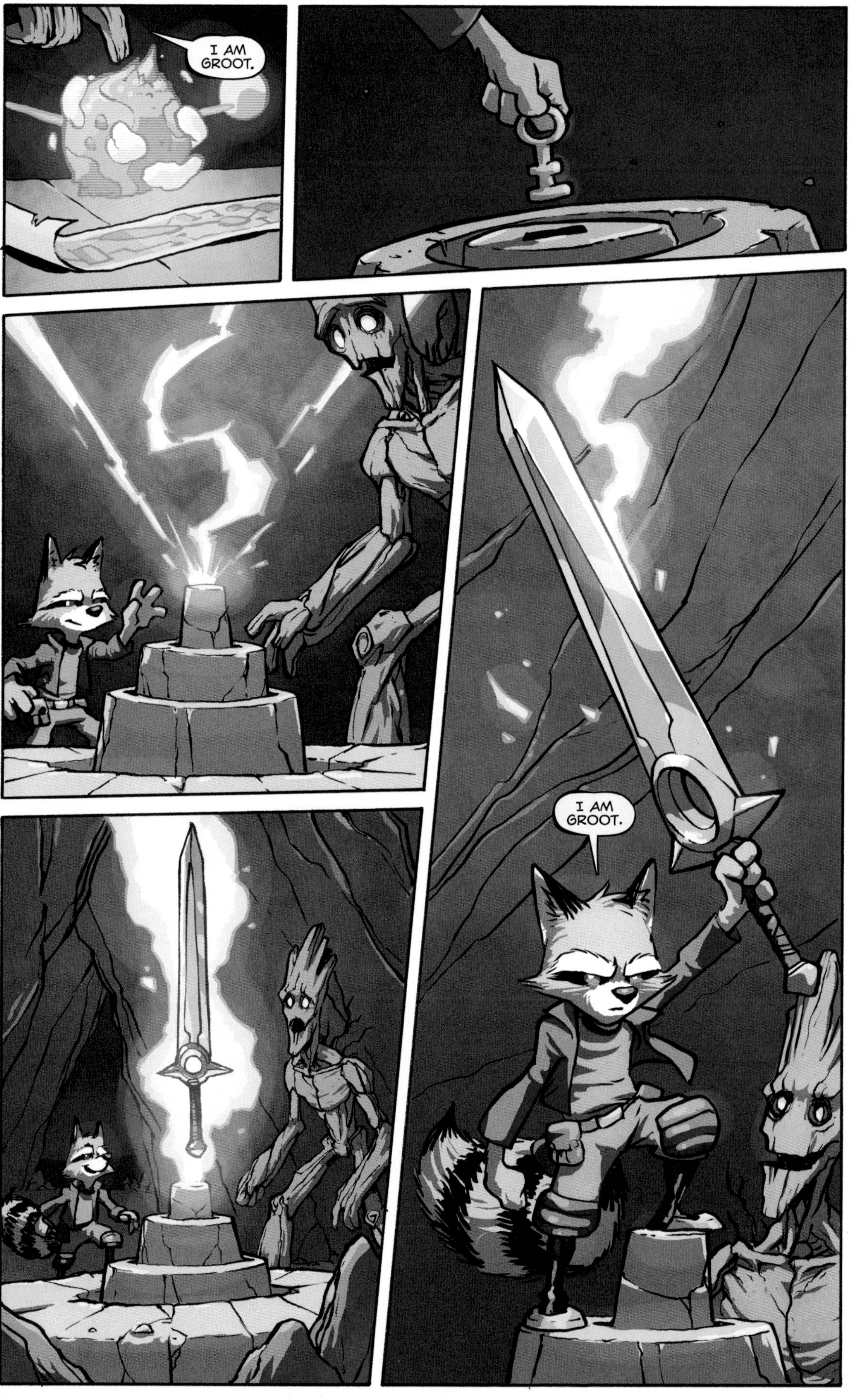
I AM GROOT.
I AM GROOT.

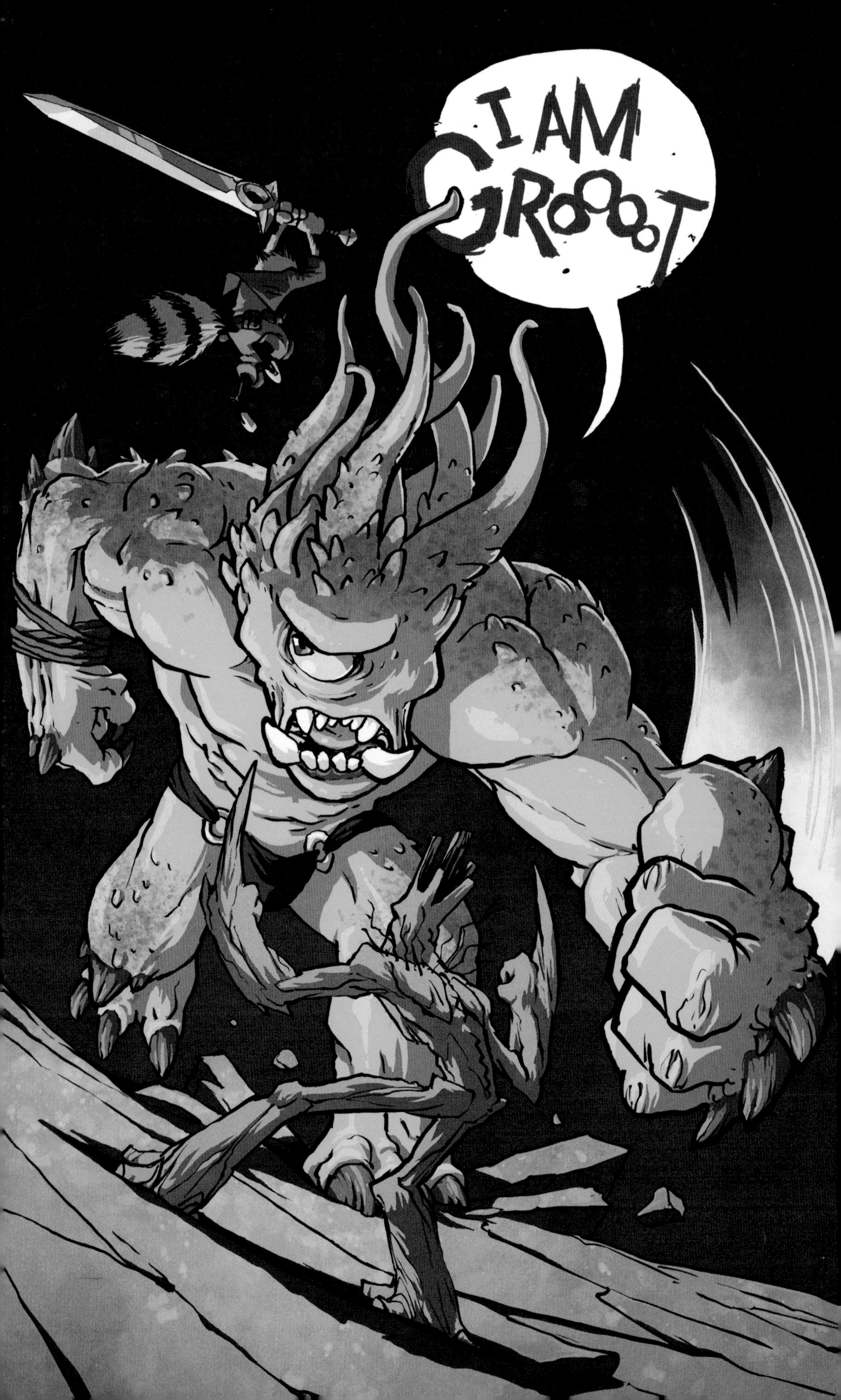
I AM GROOOOT

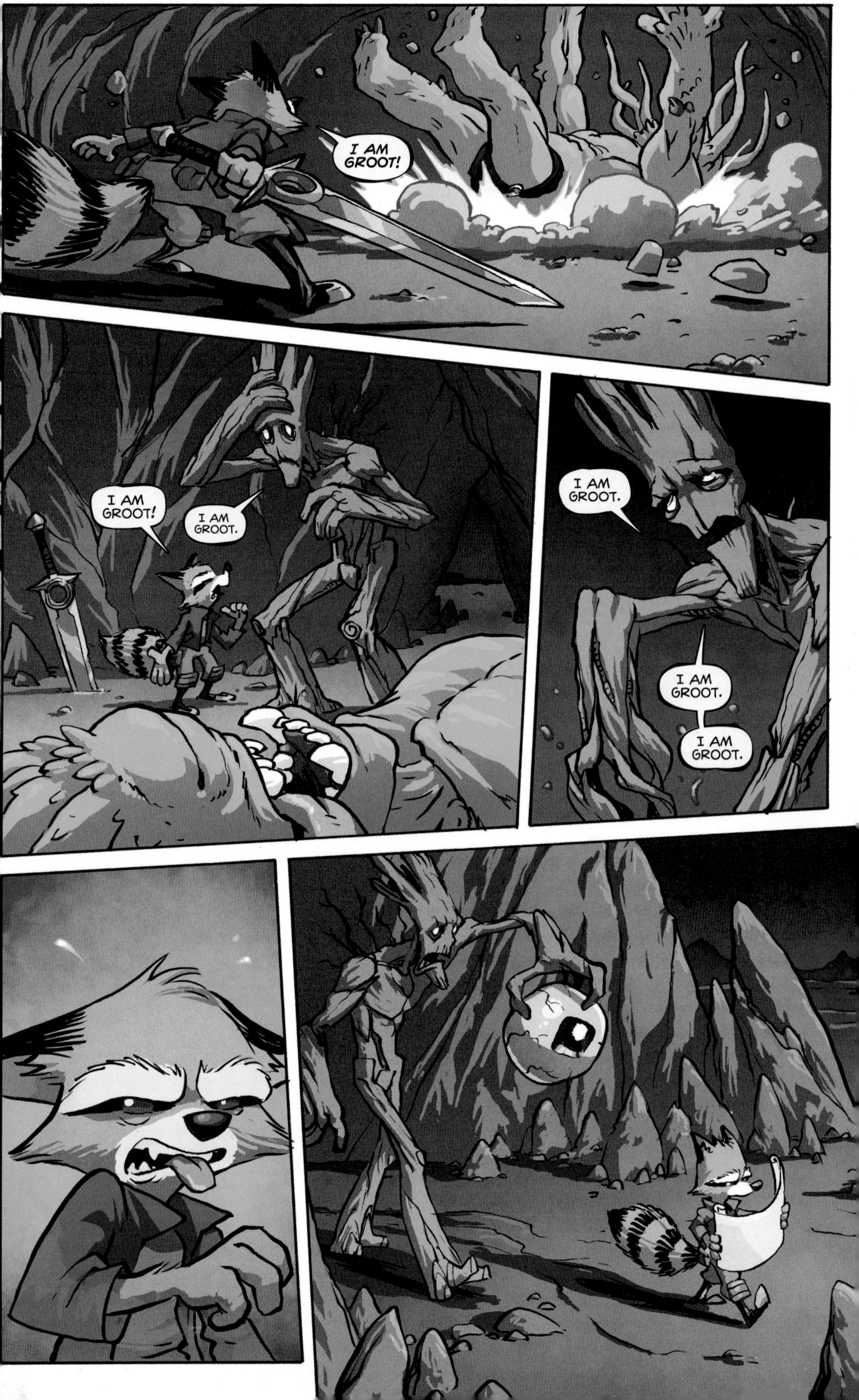
I AM GROOT!
I AM GROOT!
I AM GROOT.
I AM GROOT.
I AM GROOT.
I AM GROOT.

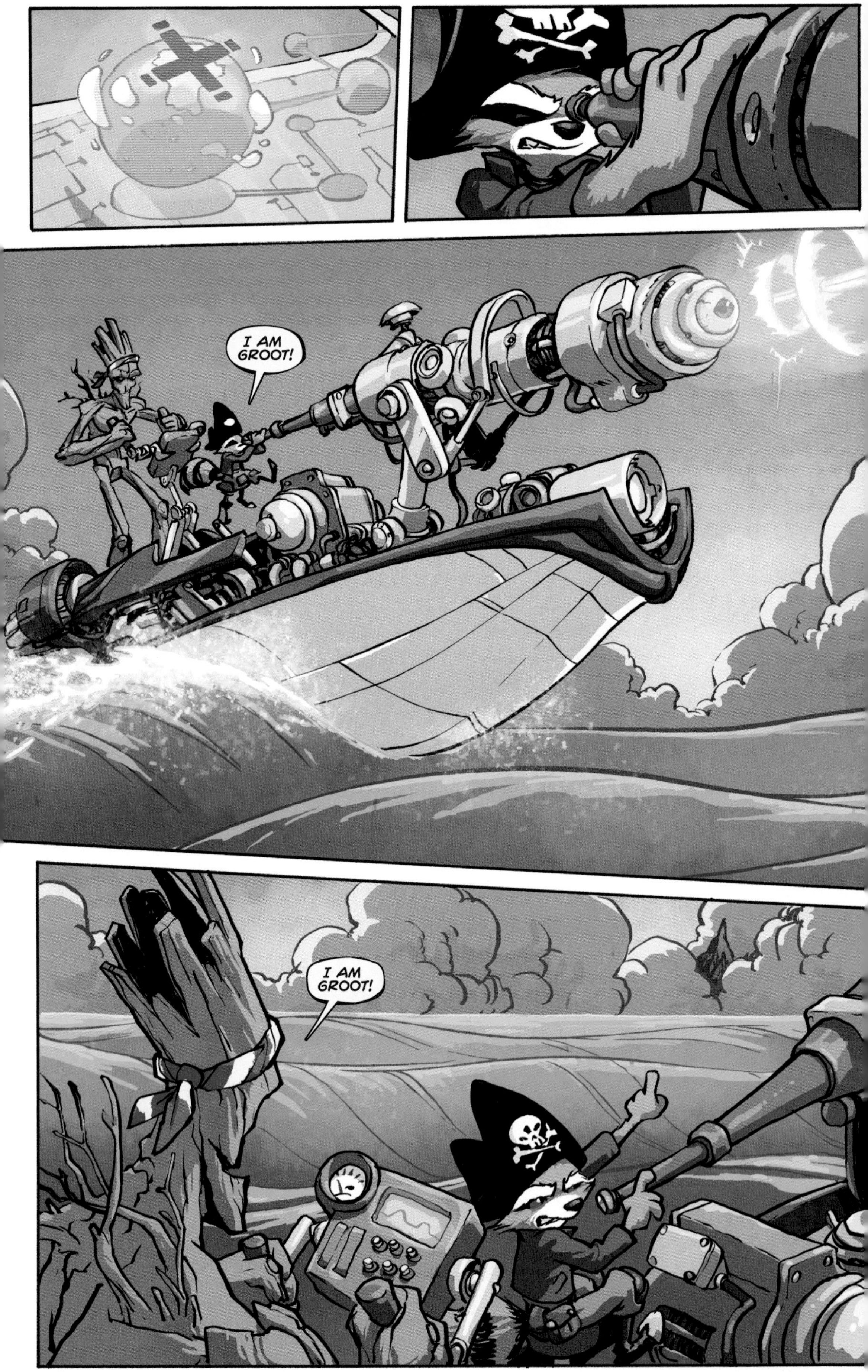
I AM GROOT!
I AM GROOT!

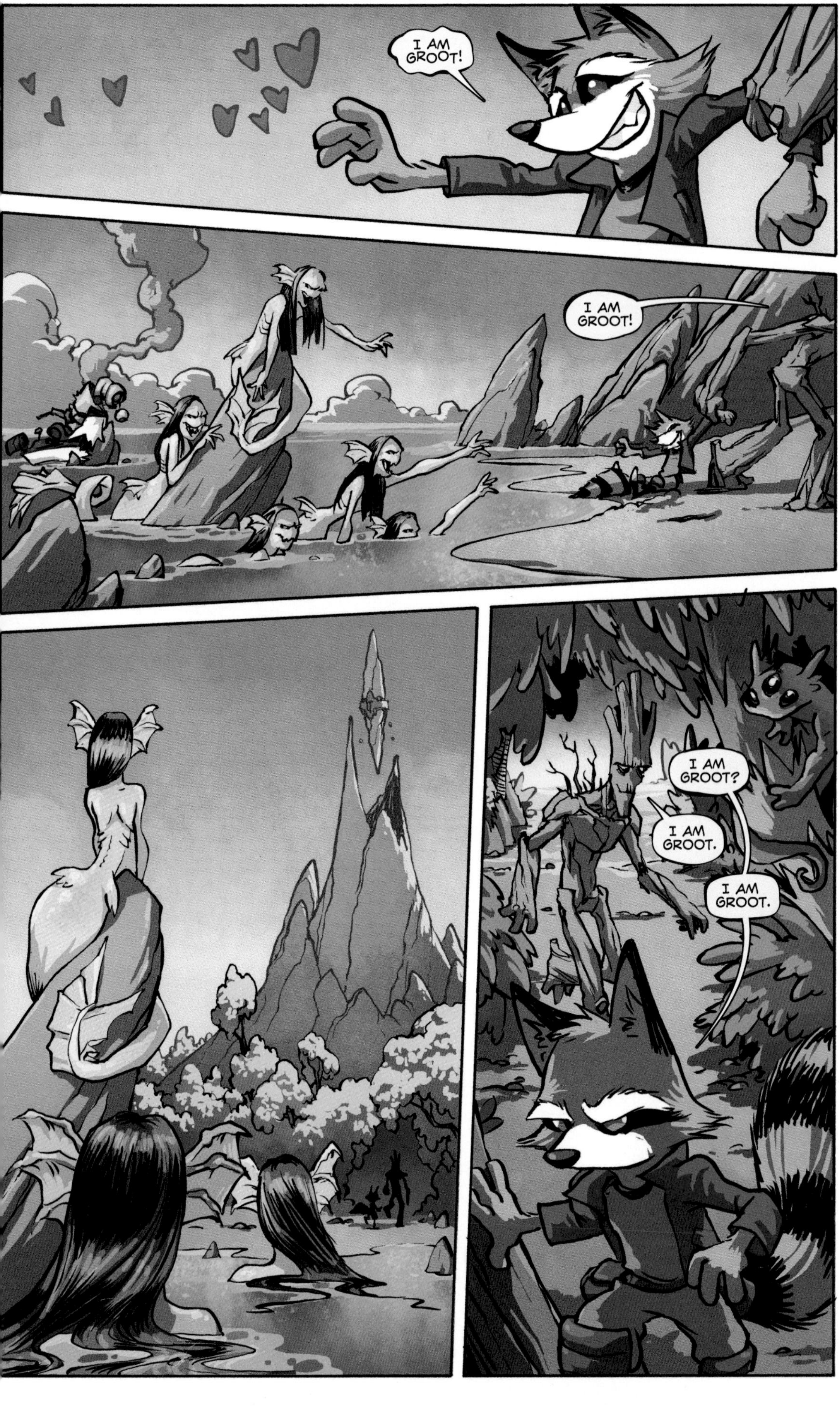
I AM GROOT!
I AM GROOT!
I AM GROOT?
I AM GROOT.
I AM GROOT.

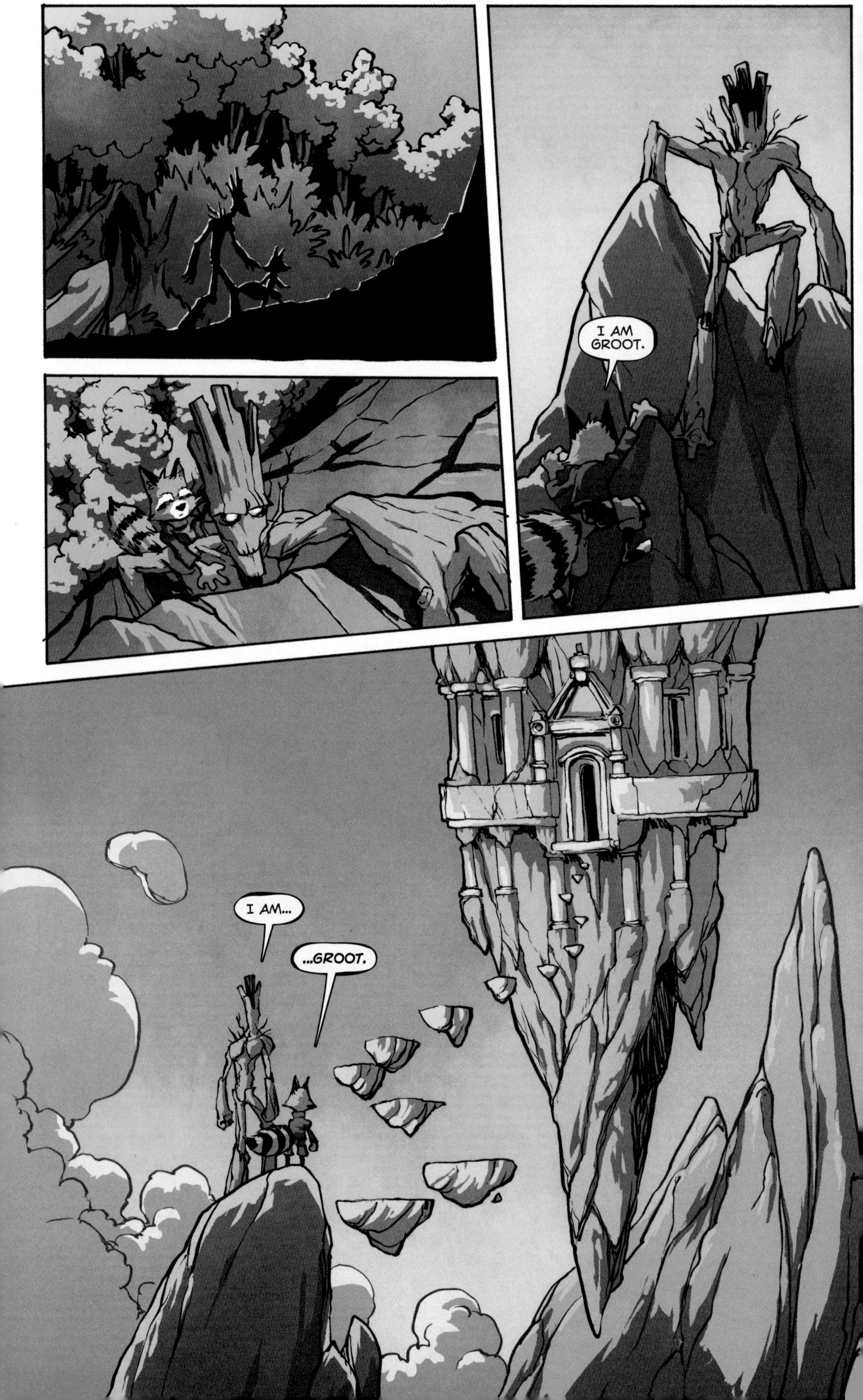
I AM GROOT.
I AM...
...GROOT.

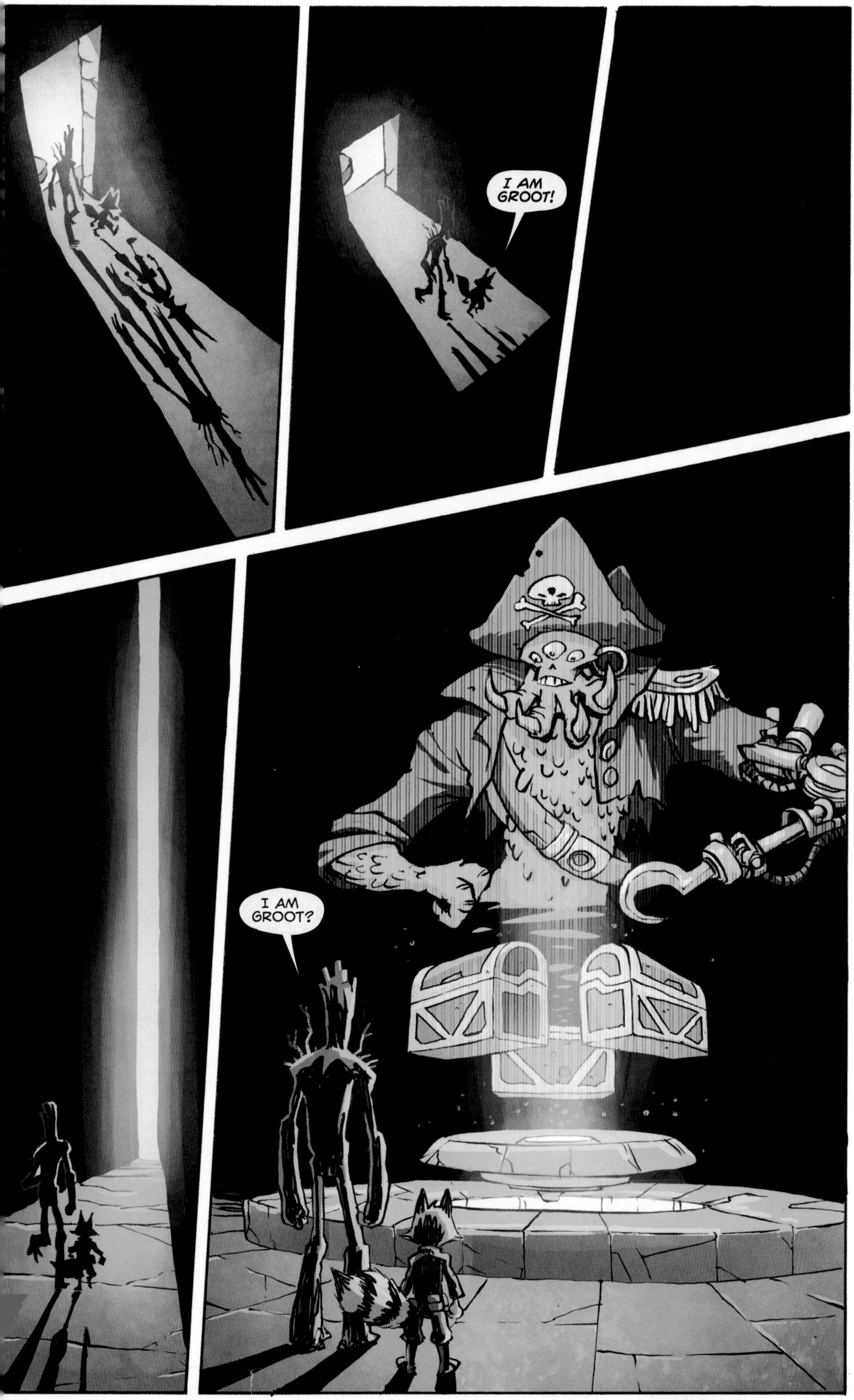
I AM GROOT!
I AM GROOT?

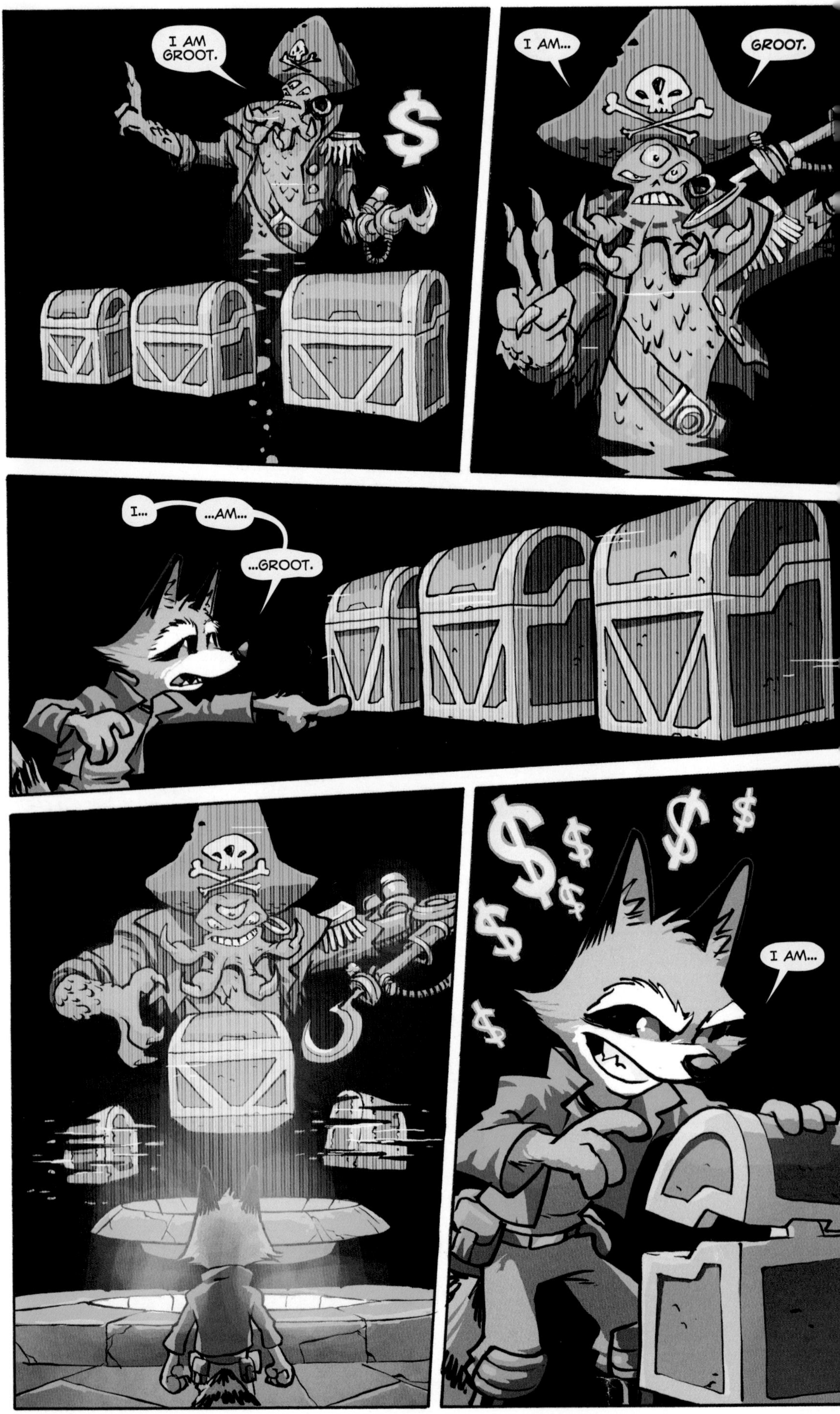
I AM GROOT.
I AM...
GROOT.
I...
...AM...
...GROOT.
I AM...

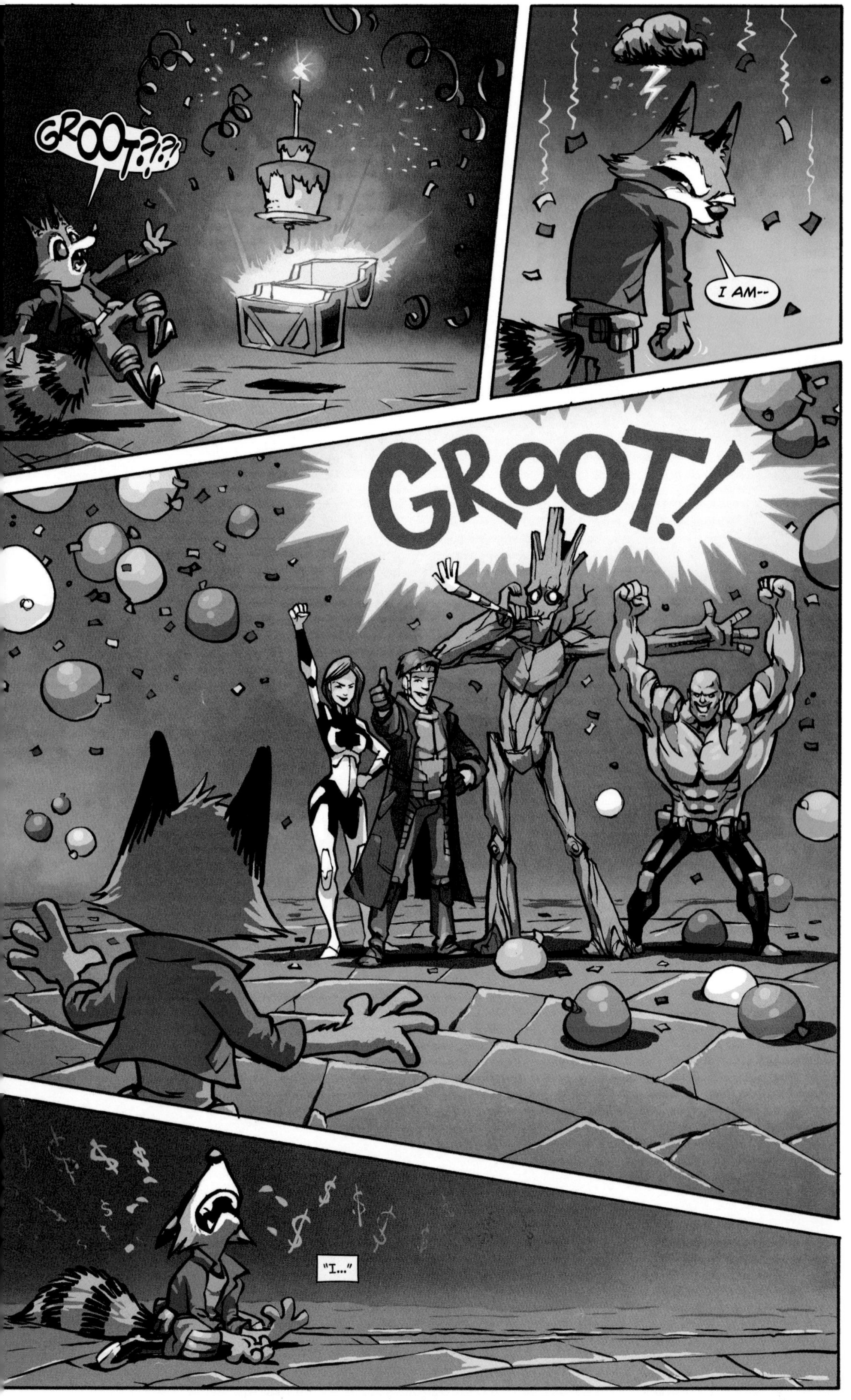
GROOT?!?!
I AM--
GROOT!
"I..."

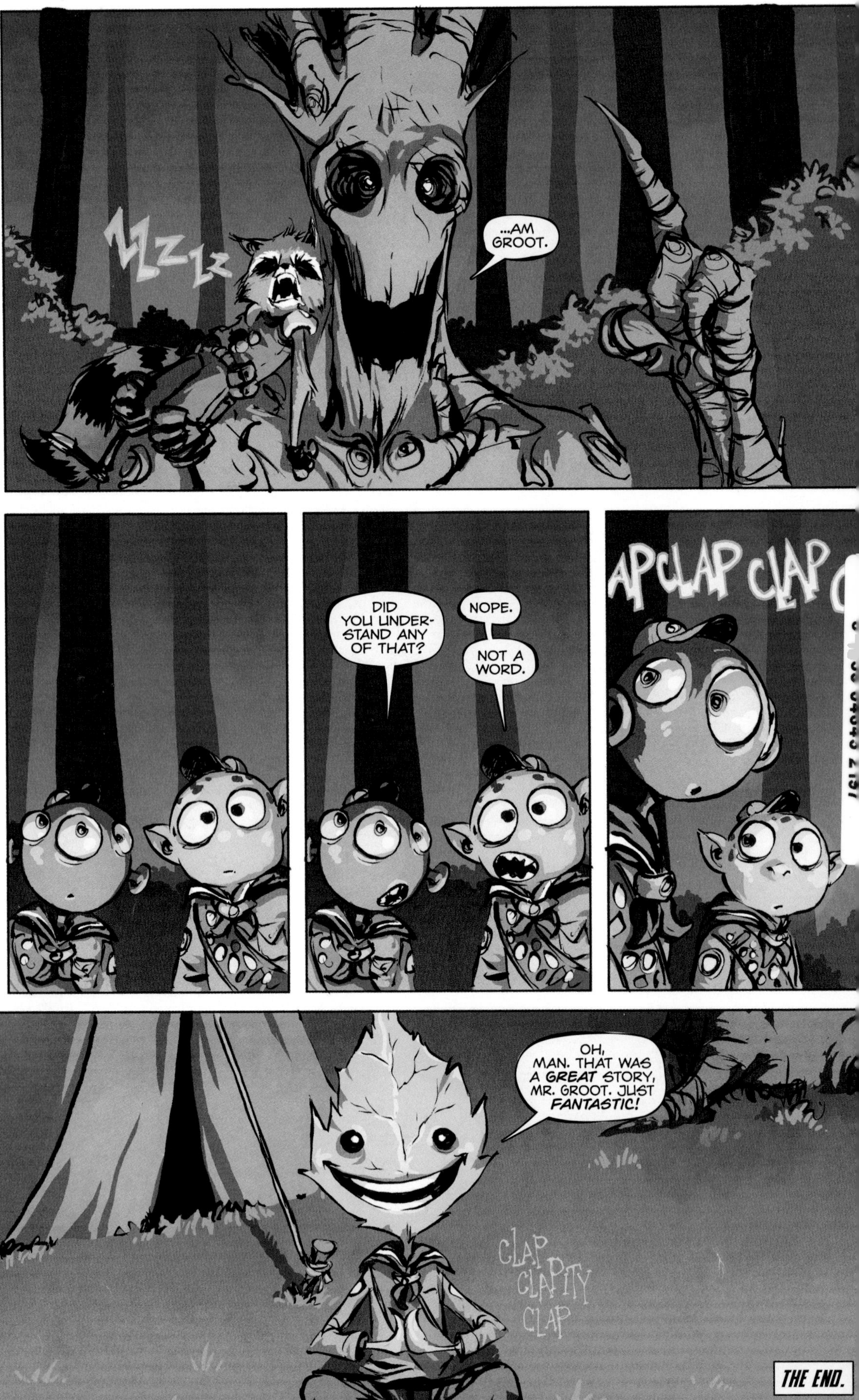

...AM GROOT.
DID YOU UNDER-STAND ANY OF THAT?
NOPE.
NOT A WORD.
AP CLAP CLAP
OH, MAN. THAT WAS A *GREAT* STORY, MR. GROOT. JUST *FANTASTIC!*
CLAP CLAPITY CLAP
THE END.